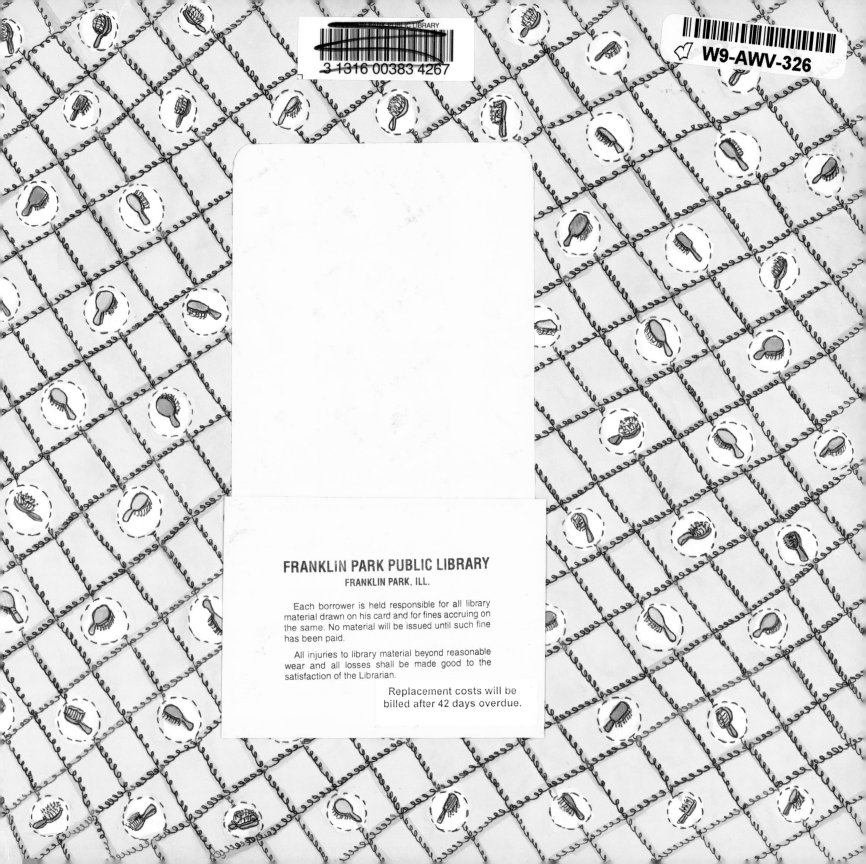

Ella Kazoo

Will NOT Brush Her Hair

Lee Fox

illustrated by

Jennifer Plecas

Walker & Company New York

For my wonderful son, Angus —L. F.

For Doris and Maja —J. P.

E
383-4267

Text copyright © 2007 by Lee Fox
Illustrations copyright © 2010 by Jennifer Plecas

First published in 2007 by Hachette Livre Australia Pty Ltd.
Published in the United States of America in January 2010 by Walker Publishing Company, Inc.
Visit Walker & Company's Web site at www.bloomsburykids.com

For information about permission to reproduce selections from this book, write to
Permissions, Walker & Company, 175 Fifth Avenue, New York, New York 10010

Library of Congress Cataloging-in-Publication Data
Fox, Lee.
Ella Kazoo will not brush her hair / Lee Fox ; illustrated by Jennifer Plecas.
p.   cm.
Summary: A little girl refuses to brush her hair until it becomes so unruly that it takes over everything.
ISBN: 978-0-8027-8836-8 (hardcover) · ISBN: 978-0-8027-8755-2 (reinforced)
[1. Stories in rhyme. 2. Hair—Fiction.] I. Plecas, Jennifer, ill. II. Title.
PZ8.3.F8243El 2010   [E]—dc22   2009013329

Art created with ink and watercolor
Typeset in Hank BT Roman
Book design by Danielle Delaney

Printed in China by Printplus Limited, Shenzhen, Guangdong
2 4 6 8 10 9 7 5 3 (hardcover)
2 4 6 8 10 9 7 5 3 1 (reinforced)

Ella Kazoo will not brush her hair.

She hides in the cupboard and under the stair.

She roars at her mom like a big growly bear.

She whines and she moans and she howls in despair,

but Ella Kazoo will not brush her hair.

Ella Kazoo will not brush her locks.

She stashes the brush in the drawer with her socks.

She covers it well in the garden with rocks.
Her mother has called her a sly little fox,
but Ella Kazoo will not brush her locks!

Ella Kazoo will not brush her mane.

Her mom says, "Oh, Ella, you can be a pain!"

But she just runs off like a swift hurricane . . .

. . . to dance in the sunshine

and skip in the rain,

but Ella Kazoo will not brush her mane!

Ella Kazoo will not brush her mop.
It looks like her head has a bird's nest on top.

Her mom cries, "Oh, Ella, this just has to stop!"
And sinks to the couch with a mighty big **FLOP**,
but Ella Kazoo will not brush her mop!

Ella Kazoo will not brush her curls.
She floats in the bathtub and watches their swirls.

She puts on a dress with some earrings and pearls,
and lipstick and perfume like most other girls,
but Ella Kazoo will not brush her curls!

Ella Kazoo will not brush her frizz.
She cares not a bit how upset her mom is.

She yells and she stamps and she gets in a tizz.
Her antics could win her a job in showbiz,
but Ella Kazoo will not brush her frizz!

Ella Kazoo will not brush her tresses.
One morning they slip into some of her dresses.

They creep round a chair and slink over the table.
They climb down the stairs and they swing on the cable.

"My goodness!" cries Ella.

"This hair must be chopped . . .

or scissored or shortened or layered or lopped.
But most of all, Mother, this hair must be stopped!"

Ella Kazoo goes to the hairdresser,
whose flashy ideas simply fail to impress her.

She says, "Give me hair I won't have to untangle—
hair that won't wander and hair that won't strangle."

TRIM! SNIP! and CHOP! go the team of hairdressers. Their scissors make light of those troublesome tresses.

Ella Kazoo now brushes her hair.

No more hiding in cupboards or under the stair.

She brushes her mane and her curls and her locks.

It no longer looks like a bird's nest on top.

She brushes her frizz and she brushes her mop . . .

'cause Ella Kazoo has only one lock!

All due to a haircut, quite simple and snappy,
both mother and daughter are blissfully happy.